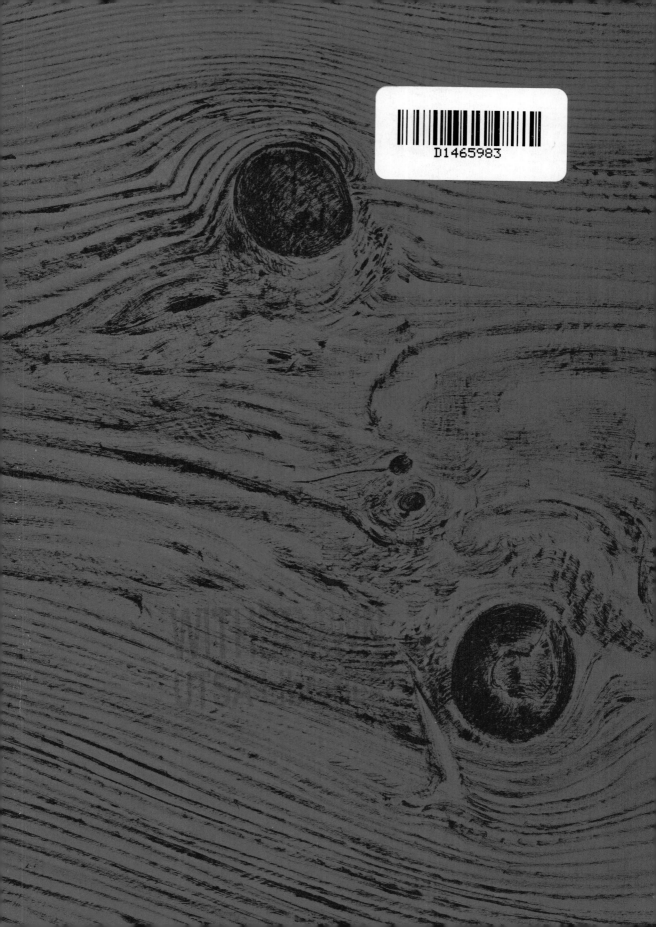

THE
BARN

THE
BARN

WRITTEN AND ILLUSTRATED BY

JOHN SCHOENHERR

An Atlantic Monthly Press Book

BOSTON   Little, Brown and Company   TORONTO

ATLANTIC-LITTLE, BROWN BOOKS
ARE PUBLISHED BY
LITTLE, BROWN AND COMPANY
IN ASSOCIATION WITH
THE ATLANTIC MONTHLY PRESS

Published simultaneously in Canada
by Little, Brown & Company (Canada) Limited

PRINTED IN THE UNITED STATES OF AMERICA

For Judith, Jennifer, and Ian

All day the sun had beaten down on the old barn.
The boards were dry and hot with many days of sun-
shine.

Inside, it was dark and cool. A skunk lay curled in
the shadows. Just before sunset, he stirred and stretched.
He was hungry.

Never before had he left the barn in daylight. Never

before had he been so hungry. He crept outside and searched under boards and stones for grubs. There were none.

He looked for mice or eggs, or even a beetle, but there were none. When he came to the spring, he found that the long drought had finally dried it up. The frogs

were gone. They had left only their tracks in the hard, cracked mud.

He snuffled and grubbed through the brown grass,

and then, under a flat stone, he began to dig. He had
found a nest of yellow jackets.

They buzzed out angrily, but the skunk's thick fur

8

protected him from their stings. He stamped on as many as he could with his front feet. He ate them, and then ate the comb with its juicy grubs.

When he had finished, he was still hungry.

10

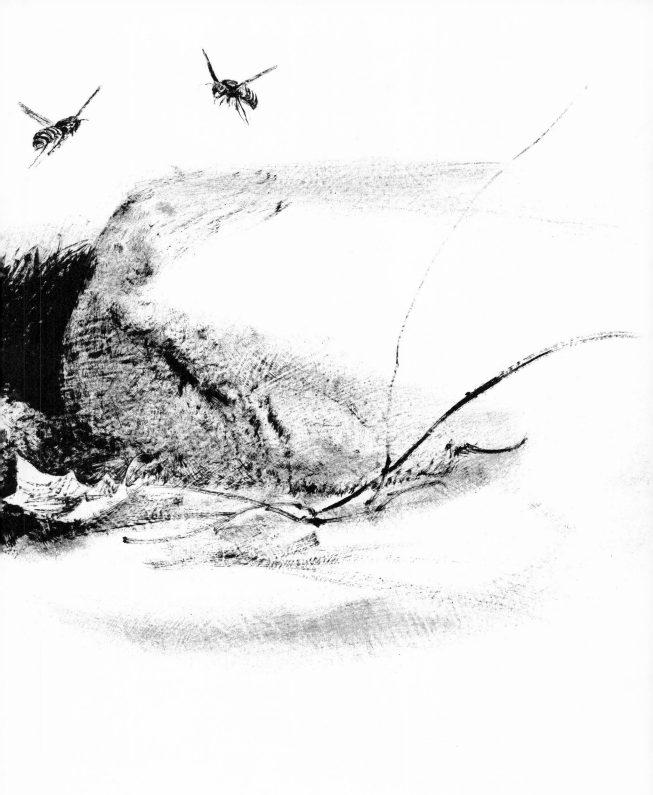

He caught the scent of a meadow mouse. He followed its trail to an old spreader that had been rusting
in the field for many years. A herd of deer was grazing
around it, but they moved aside when he approached.

Under the spreader, he found nests. They had been

empty for a long time. He sniffed and felt in the grass.
Then he saw the mouse.

He began to creep toward it. Slowly, silently. Closer
and closer he crept, as the mouse scurried back and
forth.

14

He tensed, ready to spring, when suddenly something skimmed over his head. An owl swooped past him, down, and then up with the mouse in her talons.

The skunk huddled under the spreader as the horned owl flapped her silent wings and disappeared into the darkening sky. She hurried because she had three great, downy owlets to feed. In one night they ate many mice and rats. They would eat opossums, house cats, and even skunks.

18

When he was sure the owl had gone, the skunk hurried back to the safety of the barn. Once in its dark shelter, he remembered his hunger. He saw a mouse run up a plank. Very carefully he walked up the plank after it, up toward the loft.

He searched patiently among the clutter of the loft
until he found it. The mouse was eating seeds.

The skunk stiffened. His nose twitched. He sensed something coming at him from the rafters. The owl was in the barn.

24

He dove out of reach beneath a box, turned his tail
toward the owl, and sprayed his terrible stench.

The owl blinked her eyes and hopped toward him.
She could smell nothing, not even skunk.

28

He sprayed the owl twice more, and ran around a barrel. She followed and he tried to spray again. His scent glands were empty.

The skunk panicked and ran back across the hay toward the plank. He was less than halfway there when the owl flapped into the air and dove at him.

He felt her talons on his tail as he scrambled through a gaping hole in the loft.

Under the hole was emptiness. He hung there, held
by the owl, high above the barn floor.

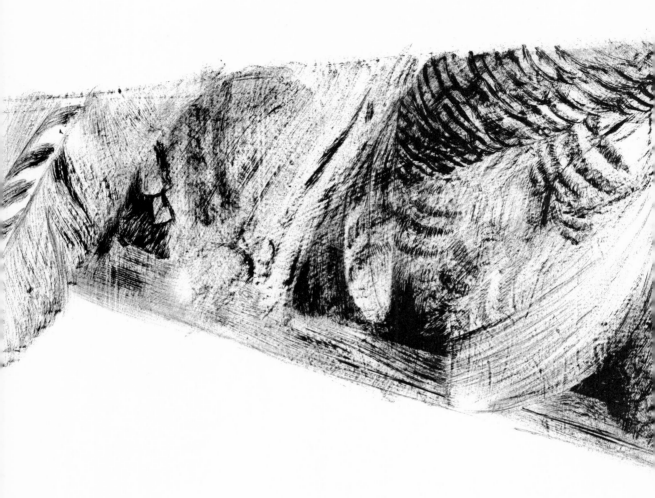

Thrashing, his feet clutched at a post. He squirmed around and up, and sank his needle teeth into the owl's leg. She squawked, flapping her wings wildly. With all his strength, the skunk pulled his tail from her talons and fell free.

He hit the floor and scrambled to the darkest corner.
He hid under a broken water trough. There he spent the
long night, motionless and wide-awake with fear.

Morning brought clouds. The clouds brought rain,

37

and the rain brought back the many small creatures that were food for the hunters. For several days the skunk stayed away from his home in the barn, and he ran from all large flying things.

39

The owl found animals that were easier to catch. Soon her owlets would be grown, and they would hunt their own mice, rats . . . and skunks.